Dear Parent:

Congratulations! Your child is taking the first steps on an exciting journey. The destination? Independent reading!

STEP INTO READING® will help your child get there. The program offers five steps to reading success. Each step includes fun stories and colorful art. There are also Step into Reading Sticker Books, Step into Reading Math Readers, Step into Reading Write-In Readers, Step into Reading Phonics Readers, and Step into Reading Phonics First Steps! Boxed Sets—a complete literacy program with something for every child.

Learning to Read, Step by Step!

Ready to Read   Preschool–Kindergarten
• big type and easy words • rhyme and rhythm • picture clues
For children who know the alphabet and are eager to begin reading.

Reading with Help   Preschool–Grade 1
• basic vocabulary • short sentences • simple stories
For children who recognize familiar words and sound out new words with help.

Reading on Your Own   Grades 1–3
• engaging characters • easy-to-follow plots • popular topics
For children who are ready to read on their own.

Reading Paragraphs   Grades 2–3
• challenging vocabulary • short paragraphs • exciting stories
For newly independent readers who read simple sentences with confidence.

Ready for Chapters   Grades 2–4
• chapters • longer paragraphs • full-color art
For children who want to take the plunge into chapter books but still like colorful pictures.

STEP INTO READING® is designed to give every child a successful reading experience. The grade levels are only guides. Children can progress through the steps at their own speed, developing confidence in their reading, no matter what their grade.

Remember, a lifetime love of reading starts with a single step!

For Hannah, Eliza, and Jasmine—
may you always have wings
—M.L.

To my dad on his 90th birthday,
with love
—P.S.P.

Copyright © 2006 by Mallory Loehr
Illustrations copyright © 2006 by Pamela Silin-Palmer

All rights reserved. Published in the United States by Random House Children's Books, a division of Random House, Inc., New York.

STEP INTO READING, RANDOM HOUSE, and the Random House colophon are registered trademarks of Random House, Inc.

www.randomhouse.com/kids
www.stepintoreading.com

Educators and librarians, for a variety of teaching tools, visit us at
www.randomhouse.com/teachers

Library of Congress Cataloging-in-Publication Data
Loehr, Mallory.
Unicorn wings / by Mallory Loehr ; illustrated by Pamela Silin-Palmer. — 1st ed.
   p.   cm. — (Step into reading. Step 2 book)
SUMMARY: A unicorn has a horn that can do magic, but he wishes that he had wings.
ISBN 0-375-83117-7 (pbk.) — ISBN 0-375-93117-1 (lib. bdg.)
ISBN 13: 978-0-375-83117-1 (pbk.) — ISBN 13: 978-0-375-93117-8 (lib. bdg.)
[1. Unicorns—Fiction. 2. Magic—Fiction. 3. Wings—Fiction.]
I. Silin-Palmer, Pamela, ill. II. Title. III. Series.
PZ7.L82615Uni 2006   [E]—dc22   2005019944

Printed in the United States of America
10 9 8 7 6 5 4 3 2 1
First Edition

STEP INTO READING® STEP 2

UNICORN WINGS

by Mallory Loehr

illustrated by Pamela Silin-Palmer

Random House 🏠 New York

Once there was a unicorn.

He was white
like the moon.

And his horn was magic.

It could make rainbows.

It could make
muddy water clear.

It could fix cuts
and broken bones.

But the unicorn
did not care about
his magic horn.
He wished
he had wings!

The unicorn went
to a castle.
The castle had a garden.
It was filled with flowers
and butterflies.

"I wish I had wings
like yours,"
the unicorn said
to a butterfly.
"My wings are
too tiny for you,"
said the butterfly.

The unicorn went
to the woods.
He looked up
into the trees.
Birds flew and landed
in the tree branches.

"I wish I had wings
like yours,"
the unicorn said
to a bluebird.

"My wings are
the wrong color for you,"
said the bluebird.

The unicorn went
to a pond.
Frogs jumped.
Dragonflies buzzed.

Snowy white swans
swam in the water.

"I wish I had wings
like yours,"
the unicorn said
to a swan.

But the swan just
shook her head.

The unicorn walked on.

He came to the sea.

He lay down
and fell asleep.

Something touched
the unicorn's nose.
He opened his eyes.

There was
a white horse—
with white wings!
But one of the horse's
wings drooped.
It was hurt.

The unicorn stood up.
He put his magic horn
to the horse's wing.
The wing grew strong.
It did not droop anymore.

The white horse
spread her wings.

She flew toward
the rising sun.

"I wish I had wings
like *that*,"
said the unicorn.

He looked down sadly.

He saw himself
in the water.
He had big white wings!
The unicorn stretched
his wings out wide.

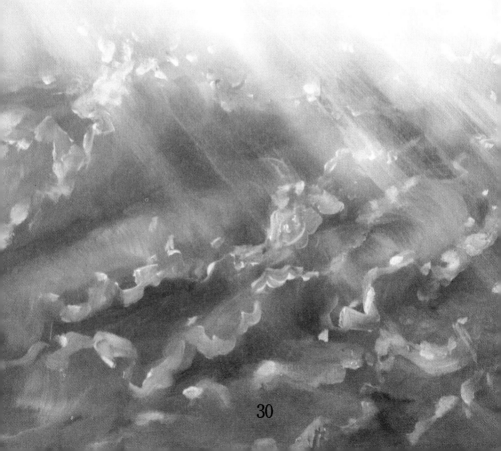

Then he flew after
the white winged horse.
The unicorn wanted
to say, "Thank you."